Words to Know Before You Read

away

fair

game

hopscotch

marbles

may

play

sandbox

swinging

whispered

www.rourkeeducationalmedia.com

Edited by Precious McKenzie
Illustrated by Anita DuFalla
Art Direction and Page Layout by Renee Brady

Library of Congress PCN Data

That's Not Fair! / Jennifer Reed
ISBN 978-1-61810-176-1 (hard cover) (alk. paper)
ISBN 978-1-61810-309-3 (soft cover)
Library of Congress Control Number: 2012936776

Rourke Educational Media
Printed in the United States of America,
North Mankato, Minnesota

rourkeeducationalmedia.com

customerservice@rourkeeducationalmedia.com • PO Box 643328 Vero Beach, Florida 32964

THAT'S NOT FAIR!

By Jennifer Reed

Illustrated by Anita DuFalla

Smokey Spaniel wanted to
play a game of Woofle Ball.

4

Tallulah Turtle and Cooper Cub picked the teams. No one picked Smokey!

5

"That's not fair!"
he whispered.

He walked over to Shirley Squirrel and Calypso Cat. They were playing hopscotch.

"May I play with you?" asked Smokey.
"We've already started the game,"
said Calypso.

"That's not fair!" he said a little louder.

He walked over to Ernest Elephant, who was playing marbles.
"May I play with you?" Smokey asked.

Mike and Spike Monkey were swinging
on the monkey bars.
"May I play with you?" asked Smokey.

"You could never keep up!" said Spike.
"That's NOT fair!" Smokey said.

Smokey sat in the sandbox.
He pushed the sand around with his feet.

14

Abby Gator ran over. "May I play with you?"
At first, Smokey said, "No!"

Abby started to walk away.
"That's not fair," she cried.

"Wait!" said Smokey.
"You may play with me."

Abby and Smokey built sandcastles and moats. They used toy dump trucks to push the sand all around.

Soon everyone wanted to play in the sandbox.

"May we play with you, Smokey?" they asked.

19

Smokey smiled. "It would only be fair!" he said.

After Reading Activities

You and the Story...

What is Smokey's problem?

How many times was Smokey left out of the games?

What did Smokey think wasn't fair?

Why did Smokey almost say no to the other animals?

How would you feel if you were Smokey?

Words You Know Now...

Find words with the long a sound.
Find a compound word. What two words make up the
compound word?

away	may
fair	play
game	sandbox
hopscotch	swinging
marbles	whispered

You Could...Be a Mime and Act Out the Story, Without Saying a Word!

- Choose who will play the different characters in the book.

- Choose a narrator. This person will read the story out loud.

- After the narrator has read a sentence, each character will act out the scene, but cannot speak. Only use your body language to show what is going on.

About the Author

Jennifer Reed teaches at a high school and often resolves problems that may not always seem fair to students. Jennifer lives in Maryland with her husband and two children. She is an award-winning children's author and has published extensively in many children's magazines. She has published over twenty-five books for children.

Ask The Author!
www.rem4students.com

About the Illustrator

Acclaimed for its versatility in style, Anita DuFalla's work has appeared in many educational books, newspaper articles, and business advertisements and on numerous posters, book and magazine covers, and even giftwraps. Anita's passion for pattern is evident in both her artwork and her collection of 400 patterned tights. She lives in the Friendship neighborhood of Pittsburgh, Pennsylvania with her son, Lucas.